THIS WALKER BOOK BELONGS TO:

First published 2012 by Walker Books Ltd
87 Vauxhall Walk, London SE11 5HJ

This edition published 2013

2 4 6 8 10 9 7 5 3 1

© 2012 Brun Limited

This book has been typeset in New Century Schoolbook

Printed in China

British Library Cataloguing in Publication Data:
a catalogue record for this book is available from the British Library

ISBN 978-1-4063-4533-9

www.walker.co.uk

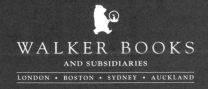

WALKER BOOKS
AND SUBSIDIARIES

LONDON · BOSTON · SYDNEY · AUCKLAND

ANTHONY BROWNE

One Gorilla

A Counting Book

1
Gorilla

2
Orang-utans

3
Chimpanzees

Mandrills

5
Baboons

6
Gibbons

7 Spider

Monkeys

8 Macaques

9

Colobus
Monkeys

10

Lemurs

All Primates.
All one family.
All my family...

And yours!

Anthony Browne

Anthony Browne is one of the most celebrated author–illustrators of his generation. Acclaimed Children's Laureate from 2009 to 2011 and winner of multiple awards – including the prestigious Kate Greenaway Medal and the much coveted Hans Christian Andersen Award – Anthony is renowned for his unique style. His work is loved around the world.

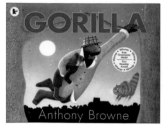

ISBN 978-1-4063-1327-7

ISBN 978-1-84428-559-4

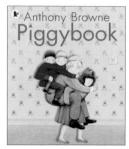

ISBN 978-1-4063-1328-4

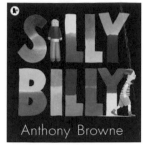

ISBN 978-1-4063-0576-0

The Tunnel
Anthony Browne

ISBN 978-1-4063-1329-1

Little Beauty

ISBN 978-1-4063-1930-9

Hansel and Gretel

ISBN 978-1-4063-1852-4

Things I Like
Anthony Browne

ISBN 978-0-7445-9858-2
ISBN 978-1-4063-2187-6
Board book edition

How Do YOU Feel?
ANTHONY BROWNE

ISBN 978-1-4063-3851-5
ISBN 978-1-4063-4791-3
Board book edition

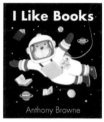

I Like Books
Anthony Browne

ISBN 978-0-7445-9857-5
ISBN 978-1-4063-2178-4
Board book edition

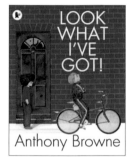

LOOK WHAT I'VE GOT!
Anthony Browne

ISBN 978-1-4063-2625-3

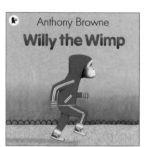

Anthony Browne
Willy the Wimp

ISBN 978-1-4063-1874-6

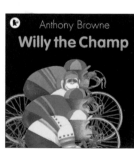

Anthony Browne
Willy the Champ

ISBN 978-1-4063-1873-9

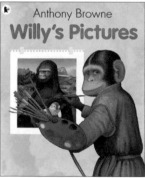

Anthony Browne
Willy's Pictures

ISBN 978-1-4063-1356-7

Anthony Browne
Willy the Dreamer

ISBN 978-1-4063-1357-4

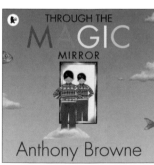

THROUGH THE MAGIC MIRROR
Anthony Browne

ISBN 978-1-4063-2628-4

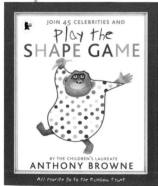

JOIN 45 CELEBRITIES AND PLAY the SHAPE GAME
BY THE CHILDREN'S LAUREATE
ANTHONY BROWNE
All Profits go to the Rainbow Trust

ISBN 978-1-4063-3131-8

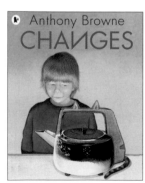

Anthony Browne
CHANGES

ISBN 978-1-4063-1339-0

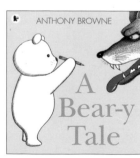

ANTHONY BROWNE
A Bear-y Tale

ISBN 978-1-4063-4162-1

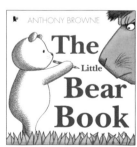

ANTHONY BROWNE
The Little Bear Book

ISBN 978-1-4063-4163-8

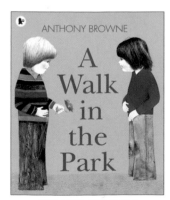

ANTHONY BROWNE
A Walk in the Park

ISBN 978-1-4063-4164-5

Available from all good booksellers

www.walker.co.uk